CAMPING

written by
Karen Hooker
illustrated by
Bruce Biddle

KAEDEN ❤ BOOKS™

My family loves to go camping.

We play at the pool and splash each other.

We ride our bikes on the bike path.

We swat a lot of bugs.

We have a campfire and toast marshmallows.

We scare each other at night on the way to the bathroom.

We sleep in our sleeping bags and dream about camping.

My family loves to go camping.